# ABSINTHE AND HEART

## THE EMPIRE RECORDS SERIES

HEATHER LAUREN

Absinthe and Heart
*A second chance romance*
The Empire Records Series
Book Four
Marcus and Grace's Story


By:
Heather Lauren

*For Ronnie My Love*

# GRACE

The sound of metal crunching and the scent of gasoline has my eyes fluttering open. It's hard to see, and my head is pounding from the blood rushing to it as I hang upside down. There's a drip on the roof of my car, and taking in my surrounding, I guess it's from my head.

Harmony, I think in a panic, but quickly remember she's at Cole and Lyla's house. She's safe. The feeling of relief is short-lived when I try to move. My leg explodes in pain so intense I almost pass out. Stars blur my vision. I scream out in pain, but there's no response.

I assess my situation, knowing I need to get out of here. Another driver must have hit me. Or did I fall asleep? Did I hurt anyone? Frantically I look out of each window, but I can't see much. The front of my mini is smashed against my side, pinning my left leg under its weight.

"Hello? Is anyone there?" I yell as loud as possible, but it comes out strangled and weak.

I remember getting off work at the hospital and stopping at the red light by Airfield Rd, then nothing after that.

Smoke billows out around me. My chest hurts, and it's hard to breathe. I smell gas and hear the sound of something dripping nearby.

Looking around for my cell phone is physically painful. Most of my belongings are scattered across the roof above me, out of reach. I spot my neon pink phone case, but it's a painful stretch away.

"Help!" I cry into the night air.

As the adrenaline and shock wear off, the pain creeps in. Dots of blood paint my palms, and my head feels like it could split in two at any second. My leg feels like it's on fire from the inside out.

I take a deep breath and scream my frustration, then wipe my hands over my nurse scrubs, pushing aside the debris to reach my phone. My leg is still pinned under the steering wheel, keeping me from escaping out the broken window. I hear a pop from under my hood, and suddenly, it feels warmer. Frantically, I reach for my phone, stretching as my body protests, but I reach it and swipe it open.

"9-1-1, what is your emergency." Tears spring to my eyes at the voice on the other end.

"Car crash, Airfield Rd...." I say into the phone, my eyes suddenly feel heavy, and muffled words are coming through the phone line. I try to focus, but the world goes black.

---

THE PAIN IS GONE, and my head feels light. It's warm wherever I am. It smells familiar, safe, and musky. My eyes flutter open as my brain starts to remember. The crash, being upside down, calling 9-1-1.

"Marcus?" I ask in surprise when I find my ex asleep next to me in my hospital bed. He wakes, unwrapping himself from around me. He's pressed against me, still dressed in black dress pants and a now very wrinkled blue button-down.

"Hey. You're awake," he says, then yells for a doctor, the sound making my head split in two. "God, I'm sorry Grace. Are you ok? Does anything hurt? How does your ankle feel?"

"My ankle?" I look down at the bed pulling the blanket off and finding my leg in a bright pink cast below the knee and over my foot.

"Harmony? Where is she? Is she ok? Did you get her?"

"Shh. Lie back. Our girl is fine. She's getting coffee with Cole and Lyla. They should be back any minute. How are you feeling?"

I take a deep breath and lay my now pounding head back against the pillow, letting it out and attempting to relax. A feat that would be easier if Marcus wasn't so close, smelling like warm musk and bad decisions.

"Confused. Disoriented."

"That's to be expected. You hit your head really hard. They were worried you wouldn't wake up, but I knew you were too strong and stubborn not to."

His voice is filled with affection, and when I turn to look at him, I instantly regret it. His eyes are filled with fear as he looks back at me. Tortured and dark, those brown eyes stare at me like I'm the center of his world. I'm not, and I know it, but I let myself fall into him for this moment. Tears fill my eyes, and he leans in, wrapping his large arms around me, and just like always, I feel safe, warm, protected, and right. It's that feeling that tortures me every day. How right it feels to be with him, even knowing I get so little of him. It hurts every single time.

"Mommy!"

The two of us part, and I wipe my eyes and plaster on a fake smile for my daughter.

"Baby girl!" My voice breaks.

"Are you ok Mommy? Did your checkup make you all better?"

"Yeah, baby, I'm going to be just fine."

"You broke your ankle, and Daddy let me pick out the color of your cast."

"And I love it. Thank you for picking my favorite color," I tell her as I squeeze her tight, sending a pain-filled thank you to god that she wasn't in the car with me.

"My car? Is it totaled?" I look up at Marcus.

He doesn't answer, just nods at me with haunted eyes.

"She's awake!" Lyla says, coming into the room with her husband.

"I am. Has it been long?" I look around the room, but no one says anything.

"I can answer that question," Dr. Jake William's voice filters into the small room, now crowded with guests, one of which is still sitting in my bed like he owns me. "This isn't exactly how I thought I'd see you today, but I am glad you're awake. To answer your question, you've been out for about twelve hours. I can go into more details if you want, but…" the handsome doctor points to my daughter still on my lap, and I shake my head, understanding and appreciating his discretion.

"Thank you, Doctor. I'd appreciate having this conversation a little later if that's ok."

"Of course," he nods, tucking my metal chart under his arm. "So, aside from waking up disoriented, how are you feeling?"

I smile politely at my coworker and shrug, "Doing ok, I guess."

"Good. I'll send Sally Ann in to check on you. Most of the staff have been waiting patiently for you to wake, but not too many visitors, ok? You really need to rest," he says, looking around the room.

Willow bursts into the room at that exact moment, and I can't help but laugh at her timing. Right now, she's frantic. Plus, there's nothing calm or subtle about my blue-haired friend.

"Oh my god, I was only gone for a quick shower. I swear I've been here the whole time… oh god, I'm gonna cry. I'm so sorry Grace." She burst into tears as soon as she reaches me. Harmony still on my lap, she takes us both in a huge hug.

I rub her back to assure her. "I'm ok."

Her face is clear of makeup as she wipes the tears away, looking at Harmony. "Yeah, I totally knew that," she jokes for my daughter's benefit, but when her eyes meet mine, I know my car accident really hit her hard. It's a trigger for her, having survived a traumatic accident when she was a teenager.

"I'm ok, I promise. My head hurts, but that's it. I don't even feel my ankle, and that cast is gorgeous," I wink at Harmony. Assuring her is my top priority, but I don't want anyone to worry about me.

"I told Mr. Doctor that it had to be her favorite color," Harmony chirps proudly.

"I bet you did, Ms. Sassy, and you did a great job," Willow says, picking her up.

"Well, I'll let you visit and send Sally Ann in shortly, but please take it easy," Jake says, still looking concerned.

"I will, thanks."

When he leaves, my coworkers take turns bursting in and out of my room with flowers, coffee, and my favorite snacks. It feels great to be showered with so much love, and it's not just for me. Many of my friends bring small gifts for Harmony to help her keep busy under very boring circumstances. Hours pass with too much excitement until almost everyone leaves.

My Mom and Dean video call from the road. They packed up their RV and started this way after Marcus called to tell them what happened to me.

"I'm ok, guys. You don't have to come out here right now. I'll return to my old self as soon as I get out of here. No need to drop everything you're doing this second."

"Gracelin Marie Maddon, I know you are not suggesting I don't come to take care of my daughter," My mom says, and I can imagine her wringing her hands together with worry and hating that she's so far from me. This isn't new. When I decided to move out here, it was hard on all of us, mainly because I came here to get to know my biological father. Not because I didn't love Dean, I do with all my heart. He's always been my rock, the father figure I needed, and a far better man than I met when I arrived here in California, a naive country girl. Thomas Reed was not a good man. He may have had a hand in my conception, but that's where his involvement stopped. The man made me schedule an appointment at his office and gave me, his blood, a mere twenty minutes of his precious time. I left as soon as he insulted my mom.

Sawyer Maddon is a lot of things, but none are bad. She's the most amazing mother who gave my rowdy brothers and me the best life possible, growing up in rural Iowa.

"You know we just want to see you for ourselves. It would just make your mother and I rest easier if we could come to check on you," Dean says, poking his head into view and making me smile.

"Hey, Dad."

"Baby girl, if you don't want us to come now, we understand."

"No, we don't." My mother corrects him, and I can't help but laugh. There is no way of keeping them from coming, and I honestly don't want to try.

"You're more than welcome but don't come just to worry over me. I mean it."

"Of course, dear. I just want to see you. You might be all grown up and handling this all yourself like everything else, but I would feel so much better to be able to see you. I won't pester you, I swear," Mom assures me.

Dad winks into the camera, both of us knowing damn well that Sawyer Maddon is the master of worrying, but she means well.

"Then come to California and enjoy yourself while you're here. I know someone who will be thrilled to see you." I turn the camera around to Harmony as she colors a printed picture of a unicorn.

"There's my grandbaby!" Mom squeals, finally catching Harmony's attention, and she runs over, snatching my phone. The three talk for a while, and I do my best to eat some soup. My stomach is in knots, not knowing all the details of what happened, but my young and impressionable daughter hasn't left my side long enough for me to ask. Her father has also been close and unyielding in his constant staring, worry painting his features, but he remains quiet.

When everything finally calms down, Cole and Lyla offer to take Harmony home with them, and as much as he seems to hate the idea of letting her go, Marcus lets them, telling his daughter he's going to take care of me for a change.

"It's not necessary. If I need anything, the staff are here to help me."

I won't admit it now, but it's a struggle to even get to the bathroom, and I hate every minute of Marcus helping me, although I'm also forever grateful. As embarrassing as it is, I trust him and am more comfortable with him than my coworkers. He's been very demanding with everyone, which should drive me nuts, but I know things will go back to normal soon enough, so I soak it all in, barely complaining. Barely.

"I'm going to walk them out and grab Harmony's bag out of my truck. Be back in a few," he says, completely ignoring my comment.

Cole, Lyla, and my sweet daughter hug me goodbye, and I release a deep breath of relief. Too many guests, too much love, although I won't complain too much about that. And still too many questions about what really happened to me that night.

When Marcus returns, I decide to ask him instead of calling for Dr. Williams. He is an established doctor with a good reputation and staff that love him, not to mention his chiseled jawline, dark silky hair, and blue eyes you could drown in. I like him, he's nice, and he's absolutely perfect on paper.

The problem is he asked me out the night of my accident, and I told him I would think about it, even though I really don't feel that way about him. Because my stupid heart thinks it still belongs to the man swaggering in from the hallway.

Marcus is tall, burly, and has this presence that demands attention. A man who always gets what he wants, not because he's dishonest or manipulates situations for his benefit, but because he's hardworking and sincere. If he says something will get done, the man won't eat or sleep until the task is complete.

He's so passionate and throws himself into his work. It never feels good to be put last, but there aren't enough hours in the day to make everyone happy. This is also why we couldn't make our relationship work. I couldn't make him choose, so I did it for us both.

"Hungry?" He asks, bringing in a large take-out bag.

"Not really." I shrug.

"Really? 'Cause Stan packed up your favorite."

"El Pastor?"

"Of course."

"Mmm. Well, in that case, it would be rude not to try, right?"

Marcus laughs as he sets up a small picnic at the side of the hospital bed. Taco Stan is a staple in our lives and serves the best

Tacos around. Try telling any member of our merry gang of friends differently, and we'll fight you.

I take a delicious bite of pork, moaning in satisfaction.

"Good?"

"Great. So much better than soup," I admit finishing the home-made street taco in four bites.

Taco's eaten; trash discarded. I finally work up the nerve to ask the most burning question.

"Did I hurt anyone, Marcus?" I whisper. The noise from the television we aren't watching plays softly.

My question catches him off guard, and the time that passes before he answers me makes me nervous.

2

MARCUS

How she looks at me in this moment of total vulnerability guts me, breaks my heart wide open, and emotions flood my chest. Grace is a proud woman who rarely shows her pain. Stubborn is another accurate description.

I clear my throat and tell her honestly.

"Yeah, Grace, you did."

A small sob escapes her, and her eyes well with tears before I can explain. The sight has me moving to her side, pushing back the blankets to take her in my arms, where she seems to break down, sobbing into my chest. The last twelve hours have been torture. I've sat here wondering if she's ok, regretting so much, haunted by the what if's that could have been our life if things were different.

"Grace, baby, you scared us. Just us. No one else was on the road." My throat clogs with emotion, and I'm forced to clear it. "You work too hard. The police agree it was an accident because all your toxicology tests came back clean."

"Of course, they did," she says, lifting her head, sounding offended. I brace myself for the defensive Grace I've known all too well over the last six years.

"But. Working long hours at the hospital is too much for you, and listen, before you jump my ass and tell me how you can do everything and don't need anyone; just listen to me. You were on the road alone, no rain or bad weather, but the car rolled so many times, the front end wrapped around your leg, busting your ankle." I stop, my voice stolen by the images of her mangled van. She was lucky, luckier than she'll ever realize. "The fire department had to use the jaws of life to get your body out of the wreckage, Grace."

"God, Grace, you could have died." It's all too much, and I finally let the tears trail down my face. I want to be strong for her, tell her everything will be ok. She will heal with minimal damage, but if shit doesn't change, she will work herself into an early grave.

"I'm sorry," she whispers. "I'm so sorry." Then she burrows into my side as if she can't get close enough. Her small frame tucks perfectly under my arm, and I hold her tight.

My best friend and the mother of my child is worn down and tired. Even after sleeping for so long, she looks like she could easily close her eyes and pass right back out. And yet she drops the ever-present wall around her emotions and reaches up to wipe my face dry. Not hers, mine. Always the caregiver.

I stop her hand from falling away and just hold it against my cheek, closing my eyes. Relief washes over me for the first time as my worry eases. I take a deep breath, weighted with the fear of losing her. I haven't been able to eat or sleep. I'm thankful for our village of friends and family who always help with Harmony. I was so worried about how she would feel seeing her mom like this, but she seems unaffected.

Wrapped up in each other, I barely notice when night falls. Noise from outside filters in, but we stay in the moment. I reach up and return the sentiment, whipping the tears from her gorgeous face. She is so beautiful it hurts—the familiar ache in my chest returns at how rare it is to be able to hold her this way. Hell, to touch her at all is a rare gift.

"Things are going to change, Grace. They have to. You've been working too hard. You need a break. When's the last time you had a goodnight's sleep and something to eat besides vending machine snacks or macaroni and cheese?"

"I work too hard!?! That's real hypocritical, don't you think?"

"I'm taking this as a sign, Grace. No more overworking. More time taking care of the people I love and being damn grateful for them." My heart is pounding against her. Grace doesn't like being told what to do or how something will be, and she's going to put up the fight of her life, but my mind's made up. I'm going to take care of her, and she might not know it yet, but she's going to love me again.

To my utter shock, she doesn't fight me. At least not tonight. She simply nods, tears streaming down her face while she cuddles into the bed, our arms still around each other with no desire to separate. She seems to digest my words, but I also know she's exhausted.

"Get some sleep. I'm taking care of everything, including you."

Again, I expect a smart remark but don't get one. I feel her soft nod against my chest as I continue to hold her. Soon her breathing evens, her heart pounding in the rhythm drilled into my memory. As it plays its familiar tune to me, I hum a new beat. Something that comes to me so intensely that I can't help but listen. It's soft, slow, and echoes the longing in the hollow parts of my heart. But as I hum, I'm filled with hope and determination I haven't had in the past few years.

Grace might keep trying to push me away, but I'm pushing back this time. Because she's the love of my life, and I'm going to fucking marry her. Claim her as mine, in every way possible. Until then, I'll care for her and show her what every day with me will look like and when she's ready to open up to me again, she's going to let me in, and I'm never leaving.

---

THE NEXT FEW days are filled with more guests coming to bug Grace. I know they mean well, but my girl is prideful, and I can tell she hates being stuck in bed. Luckily the doctor is giving her the all-clear to go home today.

"Thank fucking God," Grace says as soon as Dr. Williams leaves.

"I'll call a car and be home cuddling my curly-haired princess in less than an hour."

She seems relieved, but if she thinks I'm just going to put her in a car and wave goodbye, she is in for an unpleasant wake-up call.

"You don't need to call a car. I'm taking you home where our daughter is waiting for us, food will be there, and I had your clothes taken to the cleaners, which should be delivered tonight as well," I announce while looking down at my phone. I also moved some of my things into her house, but I'll give her a minute before I drop that bomb.

"Really? Ok then," she clears her throat. "Thank you."

"That sounded painful," I smirk.

"What did?"

"You thanking me."

"Fuck you," she chuckles. That beautiful smile, bright with amusement.

She struggles as she tries to sit up and get out of bed.

My smile fades. I want so badly to jump up and help her, but I'm already going to be overstepping. When she finds out I've moved into her apartment, she's going to freak, then tell me all the reasons she can take care of herself and that I need to get out. She'll try to push me out, but at least I'm prepared this time. I'm also not going to listen. So I let my proud queen wiggle her cute, frustrated ass all over the hospital bed until she gets both feet to the floor.

She shoots me a self-conscious glance as she moves about the room like a wobbly penguin with her crutches, grabbing every little thing she doesn't want to leave behind and throwing it into her bottomless purse. I've already taken the flowers and gifts from her friends and family to her house, allowing me to move in a few extra things of my own.

The nurse comes in with a wheelchair that Grace reluctantly sits in, letting the nurse wheel her out.

"See, that wasn't so bad, now was it?"

"It was damn right excruciating, Sally Ann, but you're a doll, thank you. I can take it from here."

The older nurse, Sally Ann, laughs at Grace being dramatic as she helps her into the bed of my hummer. My phone chimes with a text message, but I ignore it in favor of watching Grace's body move into the seat ass first. Is it wrong to admire a body that's still healing? If it is, I send up an apology. Grace catches me and glares, assuming I'm staring at her because she's awkwardly adjusting to the seat, wincing despite her confident bravado, when the fact is, I just like looking at her.

She's always been this larger-than-life bright light, always doing or saying something to cheer me up or make Harmony laugh. Seeing her like this is so different, like hearing the Pope swear or seeing Superman bleed. Our superheroes never show that kind of vulnerability, and now I understand why. It's painful to watch.

We drive home in silence, her chin tipped in defiance the entire way. As if to tell the world she's fine even though she's anything but. Every muscle in my body wants to reach for her. Hold her and tell her it's all going to be ok, praying she'll be vulnerable with me. I crave it. It's been six years since she put those solid walls up around her heart, and I've longed to tear them down ever since.

But I stay on my side, and she stays on hers. When we reach her apartment, I park in guest parking and grab her bags while she steadies herself on a pair of crutches. She hates them. I can tell by the deep crease in her sandy brown eyebrows and that adorable fucking pout.

"You know you're cute when you pout."

She rolls her eyes at me, but I don't miss the light pink that touches her cheeks.

We make our way up in the elevator, and as soon as I open Grace's front door, we're greeted by a sound comparable to a screeching pterodactyl.

"Mommy! Daddy!"

Harmony barrels into us.

"I missed you so much little cub," Grace tells our daughter, smoothing back her dark hair in a gesture I've seen her do a million times, but this time, I capture it with my phone.

"Missed you too, Mama Bear."

"We're you good for Grandma Nora?"

"Of course, I'm an Angel."

We all laugh as she refers to herself by the nickname my mother always calls her.

"Dinner's ready. I hope you guys want lasagna." Declan comes around the corner to greet us. He takes me in a tight man hug, letting me know he's here for me too, not just for the girls. I appreciate the warm gesture more than I can express, but the way he tilts his chin and steps back makes me think he knows exactly how I feel. If anyone knows how hard it is to love a stubborn woman, it's my stepdad.

"Oh, me! I do! I'm so hungry I could eat a whole horse," Harmony says and runs off to the kitchen table.

Mom comes up with open arms and a dish towel over her shoulder. She probably cleaned the entire house so Grace wouldn't worry about a thing.

"I'm not actually hungry, but I appreciate everything. Thank you both," Grace says, stepping back from my mother's hug. Mom's hand lingers on her cheek, and I watch as an unspoken conversation passes between them.

"Marcus, help Grace upstairs to a bath, please."

"Yes, Ma'am."

"No, I am perfectly capable, thank you."

Mom and I don't listen, already accustomed to Grace trying to do it all herself and not accepting our help, but I'm already heading upstairs to drop off her bags. When I come back down, Grace is still struggling on the first step, trying to drag her crutches up with her.

I sigh heavily and pick her up behind her knees, my other arm wrapping around her back. She doesn't protest or push me away. She doesn't say anything. Grace seems defeated, a total one-eighty from her usual persona, and I know I will have to be strong enough for the both of us.

"You don't have to be strong today, baby," I tell her as I lay her down on top of her blue comforter. Our eyes lock, and her lip trembles. Still, she doesn't say anything, just stares back at me, those baby blues filled with so much she's not saying.

I drop to my knees, pull off her shoe, and set it on the floor. When I look at her, those stormy blue eyes finally calm, and a hint of a smile dances at the corner of her lip. My hands run up her legs slowly, leaving plenty of time for her to object to my touch, but she doesn't. When my fingers find the hem of her oversized sweatpants, I cautiously drag them down while grazing her hips, round ass, and thighs. I don't miss the way her breath becomes labored or that her eyes have filled with the same desire as mine. But I don't dare take this too far. I'm not here because I want to fuck Grace, but because I love her and need her to let me close to her again. I need her trust more than I need my next breath, so I'll slowly take each and every article of her clothing off and keep all of my own firmly on.

I force myself to my feet when she's down to a pair of cotton black panties and bra.

"I'll go draw your bath," I say, walking backward just to look at her.

"Good luck with that," she laughs, and when I turn around, I notice why.

"You don't have a bathtub…damn it."

"Nope."

The walk-in shower is impressive but doesn't offer her any support, not even a place to sit down, and she needs to rest as much as possible. An idea comes to mind, and I take off downstairs and out onto the balcony, grabbing the metal chair and shrugging my shoulders at my daughter, who's eating with my parents, but I don't stop to explain.

Back upstairs, I catch Grace leaning against the bathroom wall, adjusting the water. A trash bag is secured around her cast. Her soft skin seems to glow, wild blonde hair falling around her face.

"Do you want this chair?"

"Oh, yes thank you."

I place the chair over a towel so it doesn't scratch her tile and won't slip.

"Well, what mama wants, mama gets."

That makes her laugh. God, I love her laugh. She takes my arm and lets me guide her to sit in the shower. The spray instantly changes her bright blonde locks darker, each strand clinging to her body. I'm frozen in place as she slips off her bra, then pushes those black panties down her hips and past her feet.

"Will you hand me that?"

I faintly hear her question over the roaring blood in my ears as her beautiful body sits before me, bare, vulnerable, and soaking wet.

Shaking out of my stupor, I clear my throat and hand her the bright pink loofah hanging from the hook just out of her reach.

"Thank you."

"Would you like me to leave? Wash your back? Watch you wash your back?" I mutter like a fool.

"I'd like you to stay. I don't want to be alone," she says so quietly I barely hear her.

Grace could ask me to do anything, and I'd do it, but she never asks, so this is a big moment. I don't hesitate to kick off my shoes, strip down to my boxer briefs, and step inside the shower. Steam billows around us, but all I see is Grace. All I smell is her chamomile soap, and all I hear is her heavy breathing and the rhythmic downpour of the shower. I kneel again at her feet, taking the soapy sponge and running it up her left leg. Once I reach her hip, I repeat each stroke across her right leg.

"Marcus," she whispers, almost breathless.

"I could make you feel good, Grace." I lick my lips, feeling bold. "Might not take all the pain away, but I could make you feel so good you forget about it for a while."

"Yes." She nods with a longing look in her eyes, I swear I'm not imagining.

"Tell me, baby."

"I want that. Make me forget Marcus."

"What Mama wants; Mama gets," I tell her again, then press my lips to her sweet-smelling skin. I kiss her ankle, her calf, and I nibble the inside of her thigh, which earns me a gasp from her pretty little mouth. This is escalating quickly, but if it's all I can give her, I plan to ring as many orgasms out of her as possible.

Running my tongue the rest of the way up, I adjust my weight and dive into her sweet center. Her moan is loud, but I don't think about the consequences of being heard. All that's on my mind is her pleasure.

3

———

# GRACE

*L*ast Monday, my life made sense. Everything was going great. And now, the father of my child is on his knees between my legs for the first time in six years. We've come so close to crossing this line before, I don't try to fight it, no, I beg for it.

"Please, Marcus."

His dark eyes meet mine as he relentlessly flicks his tongue against my clit. His wide tongue alternating laps. My God, was it always this good? Yes, it was. I'd never forget. His talent is both a blessing and a curse because I've never been able to be with anyone else.

"Oh yes!"

I'm being loud, and I really should bite onto something because he's already got me on edge. My hips buck into his sinful mouth as I hold him by the back of his head, taking what I want like he's always told me to do. Pulling him harder against me, I grind shamelessly, empowered. I feel adored and worshiped in his hands, which no one else has ever made me feel. I've missed that.

"Yes. Fuck. Yes. Thank. You. So. Much." My words are a cry as I lose control. My mind finally stops racing and shuts off, letting my other senses take over. Every nerve ending in my body is vibrating, my sole focus being only on the man bringing me this euphoria. His

18

moan vibrates from his tongue that plunges into my sensitive center, the sensation making me scream out. In waves, I come apart above him. My legs shake at his shoulders, but he doesn't let up at my release. He gently cups his palm over my mouth because I cry out, overwhelmed with my orgasm. I fall into his arms as he stands. My muscles are going limp from the intense climax.

He picks me up effortlessly and carries me out of the shower. Using his elbow, he turns the faucet off, making me smile, still feeling the delirious afterglow of ecstasy. We're back in my bed within seconds, and he grabs a gold square from his wallet and rushes back to me. He hovers over my body, careful of my leg. We're both dripping wet, soaking the blankets. I tug and pull down his soaked boxers, and he kicks them off. His muscular arms tremble on each side of my face until he slowly lays his warm skin against mine. His long, thick length lays across my pelvis sheathed, just far enough away to long for it. Everything feels so good I moan shamelessly. Over the last six years, we've touched very little, and that's been intentional on my part because I love how he feels. Far too much.

It's dangerous…and addictive. It's been approximately three months, one week, and six, no, eight days. The memory of him kissing me at Empire Eats fills my head. It's the real reason I didn't have an answer for Dr. McDreamy, as the female population of Scripps Memorial called Jake when he asked me to dinner. Maybe if I had left with him, I wouldn't have fallen asleep at the wheel, broken my leg, and scared my ex so bad he's acting like a doting spouse instead of an estranged co-parent.

I'm doing it again, thinking of everything instead of feeling. Damn it.

"Take me, Marcus, make me forget everything but you."

With a growl against my neck, he does what I ask, rearing back his hips and sliding his thick cock inside me inch by inch. I'm breathless as he stretches me.

"Fuck I'm not going to last. You're so tight, baby, and it's been so damn long."

It's been six years, seven months, and six days. Or forty-eight hours since I thought about him this way. I know this is a mistake somewhere in the back of my mind. I'm being weak and selfish and shouldn't use him this way when I know we can't make it work…but my body isn't listening.

"Oh my god, yes."

"Tell me what you want, baby."

"Don't make me decide. Show me what I want, Marcus."

Taking my direction, Marcus grabs my wrists and pins them above my head, and without hesitation, he thrusts his hard hips. Again and again, he pounds into me with slow forceful pumps, his huge cock filling me completely. I bite my lip to keep from screaming, but it's all too much. God, I miss this. The physical high rushes through my limbs as he fucks me so hard I can't think. I don't worry or stress or blame myself. I just let him take me away.

His firm grip is relentless, but instead of fighting against him, I use it for leverage, thrusting my hips up into each of his vigorous thrusts.

He moans my name as I beg him for more. Soon his thumb is over my clit massaging me into another blissful orgasm, and when I let go, I let myself shatter under him. Releasing all my pent-up emotions. Fear, anger, and resentment are gone, released into the universe with the quaking of my walls.

Marcus is stiff as he empties inside me, face flushed with his own orgasm. The blissful high, almost too good to be true. He releases my wrists as he relaxes. I smell my chamomile body wash on his skin as he hovers over me. My mouth is greedy as he kisses me. We'll have to return to reality in a few more minutes, but for now, he's mine.

The minute doesn't last long. Harmony yells from downstairs, making us jump. We laugh, and he stumbles to get dressed, helping me into my clothing. I notice the beautiful tattoo on his arm with hearts and music notes. "I like your tattoo."

His smile is shy, almost bashful.

One of the hearts says Harmony and the other Grace and the hearts look to belong to the bears that cover his arm.

We don't talk about it, but I love it. Part of me wants to think he's never stopped loving me, but that thought is too scary to dwell on right now. Then I reluctantly allow Marcus to carry me downstairs.

"Will you read me a story, Mama?"

"Sure honey." I point to her bedroom, still in his arms. "To the princess's room, good sir."

We laugh all the way to her big king-size bed, running the whole way, me bouncing along then abruptly falling onto the fluffy pink comforter. Marcus is careful of my leg, which I greatly appreciate because the pain is returning. I probably shouldn't have asked for it so hard, but I'm so glad he didn't treat me differently. I needed it rough and *restrained*. Somehow, he knew exactly what I needed even when I didn't, then gave it to me. I've never forgotten how good he feels, but now it seems better somehow. Maybe because he held me down and took control, let me free my mind completely and just feel.

"How about Goldilocks and the Three little bears."

"What?" I ask, shaking myself out of memory lane.

"Want me to read it?" Marcus offers.

"Sure."

He looks at me with a raised brow, but I just shrug my shoulder and turn over on my side to listen to him read. He's surprised I'm letting him because this is usually something I would get defensive over. In the past, I've said no to him almost every time he's offered to do something because I wanted to do it all myself. Prove I didn't need him. Prove to who, I still don't know. Me, I suppose, but all I really did was make myself miserable and tired.

Marcus softly reads the tale of three bears while Harmony falls asleep against his side, with me on the other, still basking in my post-orgasmic high.

I can't believe that happened. When tomorrow comes, we'll have to talk about it. Restate the rules. We can't do that again. His chest vibrates under my cheek in rhythm as he reads, and soon I feel so relaxed I have to close my eyes. As my body hums with his voice, like a lullaby assuring me everything's going to be ok, I drift off.

The following day my head fills with a familiar melody and John Lennon's voice. My daughter belts out the Beatle's catchy lyrics and

Marcus backs her up. I can't help but laugh as I stretch and open my eyes. Familiar blue blankets surround me, and I realize I've been moved to my bed. I wonder if I slept alone or if he slept here with me. Rolling over, I bury my face in the pillow just in time to get caught by my daughter bursting through the door.

"Mommy!" Harmony shouts and jumps onto my bed. "What are you doing?"

"Um," I mumble, turning to look at her. "Just waking up, baby. Did you sleep ok?'"

"Yeah, I did. Dad made breakfast. Get up, sleepy head." And with that, she runs out of the room.

The smell of freshly brewed coffee makes its way to my nose, and I finally get motivated to get up, swinging my leg over the side and swiping my crutches. My body aches, but I know I need breakfast before I can take any painkillers, or it'll hurt my stomach, and I'll just end up feeling worse. After I hit the bathroom, I make my way very slowly down the stairs.

"Hey you," Marcus says with a smile when he sees me.

"Good morning." It's hard to look at his handsome face after what we did yesterday. Even cuddling in bed with Harmony is something we don't do. We can't, we'll confuse our daughter, and that's not fair. No, we need to talk.

"Your parents called, said they'd be arriving today. They said they found a spot at Mom and Declan's RV park."

"They could just stay here."

"Rooms taken." There's an edge to his voice that makes me nervous.

"No, it's not."

"Yep. I've moved in to help out."

My stomach somersaults, and my hackles rise. The familiar impulse to defend myself lashes out.

"Well, I don't need your help. It's just a broken ankle. I am perfectly capable of taking care of myself and our daughter on my own, Marcus."

He takes a deep breath before answering and glances at our daughter, who's busy eating French toast and watching Fancy Nancy, oblivious to what we're discussing, but still, we've always tried our best not to argue in front of her.

Marcus comes around the island with a plate stacked with French toast and strawberries. Is that powdered sugar? Damn it to hell. He made my favorite breakfast.

"Grace, I would never do anything to undermine you. You are the greatest mother to our daughter, and I know you're a badass queen who can do everything herself. I just want to help. Try to make it easier on you because you deserve to take it easy sometimes. You work hard, and now that you broke your leg, I can and will be here to help. I can take Harmony to music class, visit her grandparents, or swim at the beach." He holds up a finger to stop me from protesting again. "I know you can do those things too, but it would hurt you. Even with painkillers, you're supposed to be resting, not running all over town because your daughter is a social butterfly. Don't worry," he winks. "I got this."

Leaving me speechless, he lays down the plate and a cup of steaming hot coffee. I don't want to do it, I defiantly don't want it to happen, prove him right on something, but I smile as I take that first glorious sip of caffeine. That sound he's laughing at is not a moan. It was meant to be a growl because I'm not happy despite my actions. I especially hate the part of his argument where he's right and I'm wrong. I know I need to rest. It just pisses me off to be told what I can and can't do. But maybe a little help would be okay.

"Good?"

"Fine, you win this one, but it's only because of the French toast. You're not right."

"Of course not," he laughs, taking the seat between Harmony and me.

"We still need to have a serious conversation about how this is going to work."

"Sure. We can talk, but it's easy, not serious. Everything is going to be great." As he says it, my treacherous heart soars with hope, but this can't work. There is no way Marcus has changed from workaholic to

Mr. Mom. We're co-parenting, not trying to make a relationship work. Yesterday was a mistake, and although I'll never say that or regret it a single second, I know I can't let it happen again.

"Harmony, go brush your teeth if you're all done. Daddy has to get you to band practice before you're late."

Marcus smiles at my apparent acceptance of his help.

"Ok." She sings, bouncing out of her seat, French toast long gone.

"Don't even think about cleaning this up," Marcus says, leaning into me with a playful smile.

"I can't just leave it."

You don't have to. I got it. The point is you don't do anything, got it?"

"Yes, sir." I joke in a soft voice that makes him growl, and I laugh.

When Harmony returns, she blows her breath for Marcus to check, and they grab their things and get going. I get a big baby bear hug, and to my surprise, a Marcus hug too. It's not forced but still seems off. We've tried for so long to keep our distance from each other in front of our daughter. When she was in pre-school, she started asking all those dreaded questions like why do Timmy's mom and dad live together? Why does Samantha have two moms? Why does my skin look so different from Ava's? It was a long year of questions, but she's really hit her stride this year. She's excelling in everything she does, plus Marcus put her in School of Rock, where she's learning to play piano and sing. She loves heavy metal music, which worries me, but I trust Marcus, and if she loves music, I would never try to turn down that light.

Musing about the house that Marcus has done an annoyingly good job at cleaning leaves me to daydream about his mouth between my legs which is not healthy. Before the accident, I was content. I knew what my day would be like. I worked, avoided the handsome doctor Jake, and went home to my daughter. That was it. I wanted to move on, maybe go on a date or two, but it's so easy to push my wants aside, and now my life is more confusing than ever.

A knock at the front door pulls my attention, and I'm thankful for the French toast and painkillers as I wobble my ass over to answer it thinking Marcus is back from parent drop-off.

Opening the door, I'm rushed by my mother plowing inside and pulling me to her chest. The sweet smell of her perfume fills my nose and blankets me with all those warm childhood feels. Her hug is long and tight, and I have no idea how much time we're standing at the entrance when I hear Dean clear his throat. She backs away, and I see the tears running down her face.

"I got here as soon as I could. Are you ok? What hurts? Can I make you something to eat?"

"Mom, no, I'm fine. Really. Just come in."

Dad comes up and gives me a big bear hug. He's the best dad I could have ever asked for and worlds better than the man who donated his sperm. I would regret moving here to meet him, but then I wouldn't know Marcus, have Harmony, my job, and all the great people I get to call my friends, so I guess it wasn't all bad.

"How are you kiddo?"

"I've been better, but I'm surviving."

"I hope you're letting Marcus help." His stern voice gives me pause. Am I really that stubborn?

"He is," I whine defensively and wobble my way to the coach. "Mom, stop fretting. He's cleaned, stocked the fridge, and even did the laundry. Trust me, I checked."

"Well, good," she says, wringing her hands together. Mom has a tough time relaxing. After raising five children, she doesn't know what to do with all the free time she has. My little brother just left for college. My poor mother and father are stressing over the farm since none of my siblings want to take it over after working it their whole lives, but luckily Uncle Bill's sons are trying to pull enough money together to make an offer. Then it will stay in the family, and Mom and Dad can travel like they want, and all will be well in our little town of Hawkins.

"Aw, Mom, you know you don't have to take care of everyone. You're in California. Go sightseeing, shop for new boots, just get out of here. I'm fine right here with this book I've wanted to read for six months."

"But we just got here. Isn't there something we can do for you? Want us to go pick you up a few more books? Or lunch? Is there anything Harmony needs? I was hoping to see her this morning."

"Sawyer, baby. We'll see everyone later. Let's go out for a while. Let Grace rest."

"Oh right, family dinner. Ok then. We'll get out of your hair and see you all later tonight. Maybe I can help Lyla."

"Maybe," Dad says, gently touching her cheek with his knuckles.

That same love and affection they've always shared is what I wanted for myself, and the familiar ache of longing hits me in the chest. Once upon a time, I wanted that. What they have that makes everyone around them so jealous. That knowledge of knowing the other person loves you to your core. Even at your ugliest, they'll love you and stick with you and fight with you if you're being stubborn. Cook for you if you're hungry. Drag your ass out of a bar at one am after a bad harvest. They have magic. I've seen it between Nora and Declan, too, but I've let go of the hope of a second chance with Marcus. There is no way we could make it work with his lifestyle. I would turn into a jealous, possessive, and needy partner, which would break my heart because that's not what we're like. Marcus and I are best friends. If that's all I ever get, I'm ok with that. I have to be, for Harmony's sake.

4

# MARCUS

A loud, high-pitched scream wakes me. I jump out of bed, stumble to my feet, and then race down to my daughter's room. Harmony is sitting up with tears streaming down her face. The sight is enough to make anyone's heartbreak.

"It's ok, baby. It was just a dream. Daddy is here, baby girl."

She hugs me back as I pull her tight into my protective arms. Soon her body softens, and eventually, her breathing evens out.

"Feeling better?"

"Yeah."

"Was it a bad dream?"

"Yeah."

"Want to talk about it?"

"It was the elephants."

"What happened to the elephants?" I ask gently, laying down across her bed and tucking her back under her unicorn comforter. She sniffles a few times and wipes her nose on my shirt.

"The mama elephant died. Some bad man came up and…and …and he popped her."

"With a gun?"

"Yeah." She whimpers.

"I'm sorry you had to see that, honey. But I promise you're safe. Your mom is safe. She's a bear, not an elephant." I boop her nose, making her smile.

Her little arms squeeze my torso as she rubs her head on my chest.

"I wish she hadn't gotten hurt. That was so scary."

"It was, but she's ok. I promise. Your mom's the strongest woman I know, and I know a lot of strong women. Trust me when I promise you can count on her. She might need our help right now, but she'll be back to her old self soon. Now's the time we get to take care of her."

"Can I be her doctor?"

"Maybe her at-home nurse?"

"Deal."

"You got it, sweetheart." I press my lips on my daughter's head, sending up another thank you to god that she wasn't in the car with Grace and that everyone was okay.

My heart bleeds with emotions I've ignored for the past six years. Being here and falling into a routine with my two favorite girls feels too good to be true. And the way Grace gave herself to me. I'm scared to question it and regret fucking nothing. If she dares call it a mistake, I'll spank her ass. It wasn't a mistake. There isn't anything more right.

When Harmony is sound asleep, I slip out of her room. It's dark in the hallway, and when my eyes adjust, I notice a small dark form at the doorframe of Grace's room.

"Grace? Are you ok?"

"Yeah."

"You don't sound ok," I say, kneeling at her side and reaching out.

Her palm is warm against my face, and I'm surprised when I feel her lips press to mine. Wet and pillow soft. I fucking love her lips, and she's kissing me right here on the floor. It's over too quick, but it's enough to make my dick swell.

"Thank you for being here," she whispers.

I clear my throat, feeling choked with the sincerity in her words. She's being vulnerable with me, and I won't fuck this up.

"I'm always here for you."

Our lips meet again as though pulled by force and a need to

consume those lush lips I've missed every day for six years. For a moment, we devour each other. Slow and deep, we kiss, my tongue claiming her mouth the way that makes her purr. Before getting carried away, I scoop her up and off the floor, carrying her to bed. The one I want in more than I want to sign another gold record producing talent. Part of me wants to be done with everything and never come out of this apartment. That part of me has been ignoring calls and forwarding emails to my second in command at Empire, Mason.

Pulling back her blue comforter, I tuck her in and slide in next to her, loving how she tucks herself into me. Grace's body molds perfectly to mine, like an extra limb. Her head tucks perfectly under my chin, and her floral scented shampoo fills my nose. Her skin is so soft against mine.

"Remember the night we met?"

Her laugh is cute. "How could I ever forget such a momentous occasion in my life?" Her tone is sarcastic, but it was a moment that started something that changed our lives as we knew it.

"You were wearing super short cut-off shorts and a black tank top. Oh, and red lipstick." I bite my knuckle, remembering the first time I saw her. We were seventeen, hanging out on the beach at a bonfire, drinking a stale keg, and bitching about school. It was a typical Friday. I was working almost every day at Mom's record store and was really tired of being a fucking virgin.

Then I saw Grace on the opposite side of a flickering fire. The ocean waves crashed against the shore behind her. A dozen kids, some I knew, some I didn't, littered the beach with camping chairs and coolers. Someone brought a football, and a few guys were tossing it back and forth. It was a normal night, then boom. My whole life changed forever.

"You were wearing swim trunks and an old Beatles t-shirt."

"You love that t-shirt," I say, slightly offended, and squeeze her sides to make her squirm. She laughs, pushing me away.

"I do, but you admitted you smoked pot for the first time the day before and hadn't showered since. You were very honest."

We both laugh.

"Yeah, well, you were breathtaking. I was having a hard time forming normal sentences."

"I remember wanting to know what you smelled like," she laughed. "I knew I should be grossed out, but you were so hot I wanted to smell you."

"Wow, that's some stalker shit, Grace. I had no idea you were like that," I joke.

She swats at me, and I take the opportunity to grab her wrists. Gentle but purposefully, I move over her and hold her hands to the mattress above her head. The room is almost pitch black, but I make out the shadows of her beautiful face. Her breath hitches, and she bites her lip. She struggles a second.

"What are you doing?"

"Taking the lead. Making you feel good." I breathe across her lips. I keep hold of her wrists, remembering her desperate cries from before.

"Tell me you want me too, Grace. Tell me you want me to hold you down and make you come for hours. You want my big cock in your pussy, making you quake as I finger fuck that tight ass hole." My girl loves dirty talk, and I've saved up years' worth.

"Yes. Please." Glancing down, I watch her sexy as fuck hips gyrate as her sweet pussy rocks against my erection. Suddenly she stops with a gasp. "Oh no! Harmony. We have to lock the door."

I laugh and jump up to secure the bedroom door and turn on her bathroom light so I can see her better. On my way back to her, I grab her black scarf off her dresser and crawl over her body slowly.

"Do you trust me?" I ask as I remove her shirt and mine.

"Yes." She replies with zero hesitation tangling my heart in this situation which is dangerous if all this is, is sex to her.

Without another thought, I take her wrists again, my mouth feasting on the flesh of her neck and breasts. After years of longing to have her again, I'm taking my time tonight. When she bucks into my aching cock she pulls on her restrained hands.

"I've got you tonight. This body is mine, and I'm going to ring you dry," I say, biting down gently on her shoulder. Just enough to make her moan and leave light teeth marks on her skin. I want to mark her. Make her mine forever. If only she would let me keep her.

With my free hand, I work her pants down. Only letting go of her wrists long enough to get them over her cast carefully. I kiss her lips, unspoken words locked away as I take her mouth and fuck her with my tongue. My cock strains for her when she starts to beg me for more.

"More. Please, Marcus."

I give my baby want she wants. My mouth teases down her chest. Tasting each nipple and flicking them to hard peaks. When she's withering with need, on the brink of coming but not, I move lower, placing gentle kisses along her beautiful stretch marks. A deep hum vibrates through me when I reach her sweet slit and taste her arousal. Her back arches off the bed, and she moans into the pillow. My name is barely audible, but I hear it. I trace up and down with the large pad of my tongue to the very tip, plunging inside her every few strokes. She tastes the same as it did the first time I ever experienced her like this. Tonight feels both new and the beginning of something unfinished, and hope is rising in my reluctant soul.

"Fuck me! Please!"

Crawling back up her body, I take her wrists and wrap them with her scarf. It's not gentle, but it shouldn't hurt; then I hold her to the mattress.

"Be a good girl, Grace, and take what I give you."

Her eyes shine up at me, wide open. She trusts me with her pleasure, and if I'm lucky, she'll let down enough walls for me to love her.

I flip her over, face down on the mattress, and pull her hips back, ass up. Her moan lets me know she's enjoying it, and with her hands still tied, she takes a few quick slaps on her pale white cheeks. Seeing them turn red from my touch makes me hungry to claim her. My thick cock is hard and dripping with my need as I stroke myself up her crack. I love how she pushes back into me, and I reward her by running my crown up and down, hard against her clit.

"This cock is raw and ready for you, baby. Do you want me like this?"

"Condom! Oh my gosh I didn't even think about it last time, but we should use a condom again."

I freeze.

"Are you still on the pill?"

"Yes, but…"

I sit back on my ankles. Hurt, she must believe the tabloids and think I've been a man whore this whole time we've been apart. She still doesn't realize she's always been the only one for me, but she will.

"But, you think I've been with other women?"

Grace falls forward and looks over her shoulder at me.

"Haven't you?"

I shake my head. Glad I turned a light on so she could see my honesty.

"You're my first and last." My tone leaves no room for argument.

I think she laughs, but her eyes are filled with tears.

"You're my only." She blubbers, choked with emotion that matches mine. I cover her body with mine and kiss her soft skin.

Her words are more than I could have hoped for, and my chest grows tight. I never thought about Grace dating because every time it crept into my thoughts, I acted like a caveman and purposely pissed her off.

My hips start to move, my bare cock slides across her crack, and the moment rekindles as if all our heartfelt truths only turned us on more.

"If you want me to wear a condom, I will, but know this woman, I have never wanted to be inside anyone else. This body…" I pull her back up to me and talk through greeted teeth, enjoying the way her breathing picks up. "Is my perfect match in every way, and if I can't have you, I won't settle."

"Oh, Marcus, I'm sorry. I didn't know. Please yes. I want you, and if you don't fuck me now, I will cry." she whines.

I press my girth to her slick entrance.

"You don't make the decisions tonight, Mama. This pussy is mine to please," I growl into her ear and push inside her inch by inch. Pausing, I'm forced to grit my teeth and take a few slow breaths. The feel of her is too good. Moving to her clit, I massage the swollen nub in a slow, steady rhythm until I catch my breath, and soon, I'm thrusting in another inch and another until I'm hammering into her sweet cunt with years of pent-up longing. Her cries grow louder, but I've left my body. In pure euphoria, I've been lifted to another plain. I'm lost in her beauty, in the feel of her, all the sensations of my impending climax and the rush of old feelings.

"Oh, Marcus, I'm coming." And with that, fireworks go off behind my closed eyes, and I explode inside her tight pussy. Ropes of my desire pour into her as she moans into her pillow.

We come together, falling into a heap of sweaty body parts but sated and happy. She lays on my chest, catching her breath as I wait for mine to return to my body.

My black ink catches her eye as she rubs her fingers up my chest.

"I really do like your tattoo. What made you want to get it?" Her tone was accusing.

"Yeah. I'm sorry, was I supposed to ask you first?" I joke, and she laughs, slapping my abs before straddling my lap. Pulling my arm, she gets a better look at the three bears that cover my right bicep. A beautiful work of art from Willow's Tattoo Shop, Moxie Misfits. Willow's still pissed at me for not waiting for her to do it.

"Bears?" She asks, looking at me knowingly, so I simply nod. My smile is honest, and my heart is full. No matter how long it takes to earn this woman back, I'm here to do it. So when I decided to get the tattoo, it was the start of many changes in my life, starting with my career. I knew I couldn't work those long hours if I had Grace and Harmony waiting for me at home, and that's what I wanted. That was a year ago. Now my schedule is mainly run by Mason my second in charge, and I've invested enough to retire. Now all I gotta do is get the girl.

"Us."

5

---

# GRACE

*E*veryone hustles around us as I work my magic, spraying pounds of hairspray on a blue mohawk for the drummer in Harmony's band. She's been practicing hard for the past month, and her dad being at home the last few weeks has given her a lot of motivation to nail it. Marcus even took us by The Empire Studio, where her favorite singers have recorded.

"One tube of heavy metal lipstick for my rock 'n roll princess," Marcus says, handing it over to our daughter, then doubling over to catch his breath.

"Thank you, Daddy!"

Her smile alone is all the thanks he needs, but he happily takes her sweet hug, squeezing her little six-year-old frame, and then stands like the run down the street to the local drug store was no big ordeal. I do not doubt he would run a thousand miles for that smile if she needed him to. He's the best dad. I'm so glad he's here. We usually trade off being at these functions so the other can work. Go figure, I turned into the workaholic I always accused him of being. Getting into a car accident and breaking my leg has brought a lot of self-reflection and I don't much like the person I've been for the last six years. I miss the young Grace who felt sexy and desired, the way Marcus is making me feel this very second. His dark eyes roam my body—that sinister tongue running along his bottom lip.

"Hey, Mama Bear."

Harmony runs off to join her band on stage, and when the coast is clear, I reply, batting my lashes playfully. "Hey, Daddy."

He comes close, and his rich musky cologne falls over me like a protective blanket. We're standing to the side of the stage behind the black curtain where no one can see us, but we keep a reasonable amount of space between us.

We look out at the kids on stage, our pride and joy standing front and center, holding her pose until the curtain rises. When it does, the song starts with the base and then builds. Our sweet Harmony belts out the lyrics to an original song the band wrote. My heart is so full of pride, tears brim.

"You're doing a great job."

I barely make out his words in the loud auditorium, but I'm happy I do. When I look over at him, I instantly feel that familiar connection. Like his soul sees mine and knows it's home. Something both familiar and exciting. Goosebumps erupt across my arms at his touch. The backs of his knuckles softly rub across mine in the dark. If anyone were to see us, most important our daughter, it would be easy to assume our actions are innocent. The slick heat between my legs; however, would disagree. This moment is anything but innocent. I've held this kind, loving, handsome man at arm's length for too long, just hurting both of us.

"I'm so sorry."

Marcus looks at me, confused a moment, but soon nods. We've been sneaking around all week avoiding any real hard topics about what this is growing between us. His smile is wide and knowing. He's been unbelievably patient with me. If I were him, I can't swear that I would have waited for me, especially with all the temptation that comes with the music industry.

"I really want to kiss you right now."

I nod eagerly. "We should talk."

"Fuck. When you say that, it sounds so sexy."

I laugh just as Harmony's song ends, and everyone in the crowd stands and cheers. Beside me, Marcus pulls a bouquet from a nearby table. The pint-size rockers stand at the front of the stage and bow a few times before running backstage, where our girl jumps into her daddy's arms. I dive in with wide arms hugging them both for a long moment. I love my little family, and although part of me is still scared of Marcus's world sucking him away again, if I get to share more moments like this with him, it's worth it.

We break away at the sound of a high-pitched whistle.

The entire Empire crew is here, plus my parents.

"Oh, Angel, you were fantastic," Nora says, coming over and joining our hug. We break apart, and all our friends and family come at us with open arms. Harmony's showered with gifts and congratulations, and we congratulate the other kids in the band. The little talent show goes on for three more acts, and we take our seats in the audience. There's something to be said about this school because each and every performance is amazing. One little boy, no older than four, belted out an opera song with a voice of a man forty years older. Needless to say, they all received standing ovations.

"Family dinner?" My dad asks the group. It's a tradition for us all to have dinner together, and over the years, it's become harder to keep my reservation with me working extra hours at the hospital, so it pains me to tell them no again.

"You guys go ahead. My painkillers are beginning to wear off, and I've been on my feet all day. I think I'll go home and rest," I admit leaning against my crutches.

"I'll take you. Harmony, do you want to come home or go to dinner with everyone and, of course, your epic sleepover with Charlie and Hudson?"

"Are you kidding? I'm too pumped to sit at home, Daddy. I have to celebrate.'"

"You are a rock star. I don't blame you," I tell her honestly, and Marcus nods his agreement. Her favorite Aunt Willow comes up from behind, making her squeal as she lifts her. I see Archer bite his lip as he watches them play, and I wonder if he's getting baby fever. The newlyweds have been "borrowing" my daughter a lot lately, and I'd bet she's already pregnant or will be soon.

"Want to ride in my new car? It's very fast?"

"No!" Marcus and I say in unison. I hear Cole and Lyla laugh at us as Willow pouts.

"Fine, but I'm taking her picture in it…driving." She says the last part softer into Harmony's ear, making me roll my eyes. I trust her with my daughter's safety and know she's mostly joking. It's the *mostly* part that worries me.

"You two want us to bring you any dinner?" My mom asks, hugging me goodbye.

"No, thank you. I'm not hungry, and if that changes, I can order take out."

"Ok, honey. We love you." No child of Sawyer Maddon would doubt that. I certainly don't.

"Love you guys, too."

Marcus and I continue all the goodbyes, ending with hugs and kisses as we buckle Harmony in Charlie's minivan. It's still crazy to think of my dear friend as a megastar, but she deserves it. I wonder if anyone in the audience realized two real-life rock stars were sitting in the crowd like commoners.

"You really don't mind her sleeping over? You guys just got off tour. You must be tired."

"Nonsense, it's great practice," Hudson answers in his thick British accent.

"He's right. Plus, we've been back for a week already, so we have the guest room set up and bought all her favorite snacks," Charlie says, starting the engine.

"We've been looking forward to this more than Harmony. I assure you love."

"Ok. Great. Hope you guys have a great night then," Marcus says and closes the sliding door.

Everyone in the van echoes their goodbyes, and we all wave goodbye as they drive off. Cole and Lyla wave from Cole's truck with mom and dad in the back, followed by Willow driving a flashy hot rod, and finally, Nora and Declan zoom past us on a motorcycle. I wobble along the uneven parking lot, the end of my crutch stepping in gum. Gross. His car isn't far, and when I finally make it to the passenger's side door, I'm surprised by his hard body pressing me against the door. Marcus growls into my ear.

"So, where would you like me to make you come?"

I gasp at his crass words and feel the heat in my cheeks without needing to look at my reflection. Speechless, I stare at him, but that cocky man just smiles back and helps me into his Hummer. While he's making his way around to the driver's side, I take a minute and really think about his question. Where? Anywhere as long as it's him. The voice inside me that usually says no to any alone time with Marcus is dead silent, leaving me to fight the growing urges on my own.

We've been with Harmony most of the day and forced to behave. The man beside me is no help as he jumps in and sets off, pulling onto the main road, and then places a possessive hand on my thigh. I've missed his hand's warmth, and it's now trailing up the peak of my yoga pants.

"Want to come to my place tonight since the rock stars are having a sleepover?"

"Yeah, sure." I try to sound casual, but inside I'm an inferno. His sly pinky slides up and nudges my nub.

"Just got one stop to make, and then we can swing by your place and grab whatever you want."

I nod with excitement, giant moths in my stomach taking flight. Even after all these years, this man excites me like no other. It's like I'm seventeen again and sneaking off to fool around. It feels both dangerous and thrilling, along with other things I haven't felt in a very long time.

My chest burns with it. History. But I won't think about that right now. Tonight feels different somehow. Something all new and full of possibilities. So I clutch onto that thought and ignore the heavy weight of our past. Instead, I watch his ass, clad in black dress pants, full of sexy swagger, as he walks into a liquor store.

FINALLY, at his place, I find a giant black recliner and hobble over, leaving my crutches at the door.

"Ok, ready for your surprise?"

I nod eagerly, grinning and wide-eyed like a kid, but I'm shocked when he pulls out a large glass bottle with neon green liquid.

"Oh no, you didn't."

"I might have," he tells me with a devilish grin.

Marcus moves around his kitchen, and I take a moment to look around. What has changed about this man that I don't know about? The question makes me hungry for the answer, but when my eyes stop scanning the room and fall on a photo hanging on the wall, I'm frozen. My chest constricts, and I swear my heart skips a beat. A large family picture of the three of us is blown up on the wall, framed by more of us over the years. Not just Harmony, but photos of me too.

I bite back a wince as I limp over to the photos for a better look.

"You have pictures of the bonfire?"

That was the first night we met. My question doesn't surprise him. He calmly comes over to me with an outstretched cocktail glass containing the glowing green elixir.

"I broke into the art department where the yearbook kids had their little meeting, and I knew they'd have the picture." He shrugs.

"You did what? When?"

"Senior year. I politely asked stuck-up Steven for a copy, but he got on this power trip. Long story short, I popped the lock that night and swiped every copy he had plus the negative. Take that, Steven," Marcus jokes.

"But didn't Steven know it was you? Did you get caught? Also, I don't remember anyone by that name going to school with us."

"It's probably not his real name, but that's not the point."

"Don't mess with Marcus," I say in awe.

"That's right. I get what I want."

The last part is said over his shoulder, staring down at me with such an intense look of desire I almost drop to my knees. Having his full attention on me is intoxicating, like a drug.

"I've been in love with you since the moment they took that picture, you know."

At his words, I completely break. Tears choke me and brim on my eyelids. I nod, remembering the moment I felt the same way.

"You were the new girl at school, and everyone was talking about you. Someone mentioned you were going to the bonfire, so I got Lyla to cover my shift at Empire so I could meet you."

I laugh, "You stood on the other side of the fire just staring at me like a total weirdo."

"I HAD GAME BACK THEN, too. I just lost my cool around you. You're intimidating, Grace."

I shake my head, not agreeing with him but loving the honesty in his eyes. It reaffirms what I've always known and have been too stubborn to admit. I'm not fighting this happiness anymore. Life is too short.

"I love you. Maybe it happened that night, maybe later, but I fell madly, deeply, and permanently in love with you, and I'm so sorry I've been pushing you away. Holding you at arm's length."

Marcus takes me in his arms, and there I stay, feeling safe, warm, and home. Like everything is finally going to be ok. He kisses the top of my head. Seconds later, my cheek and trails down to my lips, where he takes them with his.

6

## MARCUS

"*I* love you, too."

My mouth trails down her soft neck. She smells like chamomile and tastes like cotton candy. I lick her collarbone and across her cheek. My eager hands grip her breasts, making her squirm. I feel my way down her sides and over her hips. In a sharp pull, her legs are wrapped around my waist, and her crutches fall to the floor. We don't stop to care. I carry her in my arms down the wall and into my bedroom.

"I've been thinking about you all day. Watching you and not being able to touch you is getting to be too hard for me."

"What are you saying?" I ask, laying her down on my white comforter. The bathroom light provides a low glow making her blonde hair shine around her like a fucking goddess.

"I want to be official. Tell everyone. Go out together."

"Be my date for snotty celebrity events you'll likely hate?"

"Yes, it's still worth it if I'm with you."

"I hope you mean that, Grace. Because I will do anything, sacrifice anything for our family. For you, for Harmony, I would give every-thing up just to keep you safe. To make sure I can be the present husband you deserve and not the constantly distracted boyfriend I used to be."

Her gasp is audible, but I don't regret it. This isn't a proposal because I have different plans for that, but if this week has taught me anything, I'm not waiting for life to slow down before I make the changes in my life that I need to be happy.

Pushing those plans to the back of my mind for later, I take her mouth in a rushed kiss. Moving my mouth with hers as our bodies grind, teasing us both with unsatisfying friction.

Her hands pull at my shirt, and I reach back and pull it off by the collar. She slips my belt off and pushes my pants down so I can kick them off. Her yoga pants get stuck around her cast, but when I finally have her bare underneath me, I pull my surprise from the box under the bed.

"Do you trust me?"

"Of course I do. Why would you ask such a question?"

I slip the red rope between her fingers, letting her know what I'm doing.

"Because I've made you come a million times in our life together but never as hard as you came for me when I tied you up."

I'm pressed so close against her small frame. I feel the shiver that runs through her at my words. One at a time, I hold her arms together above her head.

"Is this ok?" I will stop right this second if this makes her anything but turned on.

"Yes." She nods, heaving each breath.

Focused on her every reaction, I tie her wrists together in a strong knot, nothing fancy, and lose enough for her to break free if she doesn't like this. I raise her arms above her head and hold her to the mattress. My free hand trails down her body slowly, watching the goosebumps erupt across her fair skin. The way my dark skin looks beside hers reminds me of a painting. Our love is a beautiful piece of artwork.

"Are you wet right now? Do you get slick between those beautiful legs when I take control?"

She nods at the same time my fingers trail under her underwear; I find my girl pooled with desire.

"Fuck, you're so wet for me. Give me control. I'll take care of you, baby. I got you." I slip a finger into her center and pump, slowly building speed, my rhythm in time with her cries.

"Yes."

Pulling out my finger, I align my cock and moan at the sight of it running up her glistening center. This body is as familiar to me as my own, even though it's been years.

Pushing my hard cock into her throbbing pussy, I lay across her, looking into her eyes as I make love to her. I tell her I love her with every drive of my steel cock. I show her with my body, tell her with my eyes, my mouth, and my thrusts over and over.

Her screams are loud, set free with total privacy.

When her wall begins to clinch, I stop and pull out. Her cute whine is followed by a gasp when I flip her over and pull her hips back. My cock easily slides into her, and I drive into her hard. She screams for more as I pump faster. The feeling of her exquisite body around me fuels my passion, and I hammer it back into her. She's my sun, moon, and stars, and now, after all this time, she's ready to be mine again. To accept my love, she's always had. My heart is free to start beating again. Grace told me she loves me.

My thumb moves to her puckered hole as my cock glides in and out of her sweet pussy. She doesn't even flinch. Instead, her moan fills my ears as I slide my digit inside. Filling her like this has my cock throbbing. I'm on the edge, and I need her with me.

"You are my everything, and you're going to come all over my cock when I fill this sweet pussy with my come. You are mine and always have been."

I don't recognize my own voice. The guy growling down at the love of his life as she shakes in a climax is someone new. Maybe someone I've always been, but this version of me has been asleep for the past six years. Lack of sex starved me, and now that I've had Grace again, the beast inside me is unleashed. My hips piston into her tight wet pussy furiously. Our bodies are slick with a sheen of sweat, our bodies slapping together with a sound so filthy I wish I was recording it. Music better than any beat I've ever created.

Suddenly I'm gushing, filling my girl with ropes of come, years' worth of longing and empty fantasies spilling inside her perfect pussy.

Both of us gasping for breath, we fall to the mattress spent. I slip out of her gently and kiss her shoulder. Grazing her sensitive skin with my teeth, I bite. Just hard enough to leave my print and make her moan.

"You're unbelievable," I say, kissing her forehead, unable to stop touching her. Our slick bodies slide together perfectly like the missing puzzle piece found slightly damaged, but when it's back home, it makes a beautiful masterpiece.

I take her wrists and untie the rope, kissing the pink imprints on her skin.

"You are."

The look on her face makes my chest grow tight with emotion. I can feel tears sting my eyes as I clear my throat.

"I love you, Grace. You'll never truly know how that felt. Not just the mind-blowing orgasm," I joke, "But you giving me control. Giving me the chance to prove I'll take care of you. That's what I've always wanted for us. To be equal. Not just about me and my career and you just handling everything like it was before we got pregnant. But not like it has been the last few years either with you carrying the weight of the world and not letting me into yours. I want to share our lives, not just co-exist co-parenting. I want our family, our perfect family, to live under one roof."

There's a long pause, and the room grows quiet until she finally jokes, "Are you trying to get lucky again because I'm going to need a minute?"

I laugh at her playful tone and see the twinkle in her eye. Hear the emotion in her voice, so I kiss her. Run my fingers over her soft skin and just take in the moment. All of it. What we just did, and how this feels like something new and bigger than ever before.

We lay together in silence, just enjoying the feel of our skin against each other. Her golden curls fall like silk through my fingers; the moment is calm, the opposite of just ten minutes earlier. Those sweet lips of hers are raw, swollen from my mouth.

"I'll shave my beard," I say, gently touching her sexy pout.

"Shave what beard? It's so short, plus I kinda like it."

"Oh, in that case, never mind. Here I thought it hurt you to kiss me."

"I thought it would, but it actually turns out kissing you is a better feeling than almost anything else. And if you haven't noticed, I like it a little rough."

With a sexy wink, she gets up and heads to the bathroom.

"The beard stays!"

"The beard definitely stays, and the rope!" She hollers back over her shoulder.

"Fuck!" I growl, biting my knuckle. I think Grace and I have found something special with this new kink. Something better than couple's counseling.

I quickly clean up and grab an extra t-shirt for my girl. It feels good to put that title back on her without having to tell myself to keep dreaming. I'm not just wishing for her back; she's really here.

I tip-toe out of the room, leaving the shirt on my bed, and head for my record player. I easily find the right album and set it spinning. The Beatles' slow, funky melody fills the air around me as I run around lighting candles and setting up the absinthe fountain and everything to drink it with. I can hear her in the other room singing along, and I glance just in time to see her trim body engulfed in my white tee. Those silky blonde curls fall around her shoulders, and that smile beams at me as our eyes lock. I walk up to her and lift her against my chest, spinning her around and making her giggle. It's so cute, and I can't help but hold her tighter. I run my nose up the slope of hers, just breathing her in.

"Harmony has your laugh."

"Poor girl," she jokes. It's something she's never liked about herself. Her laugh is usually loud and the opposite of her name, but I love it.

"My love, you are a queen." I push back a few strands of her hair as I tell her honestly how amazing I think she is. "You're selfless and determined and super fucking stubborn, but God gave you that unique laugh to let us mere mortals know even you aren't *that* perfect."

I laugh when she scoffs at my words rearing back to leave my arms before I can explain. "Wait, I mean you are perfect, perfect for me, for Harmony, and the world loves you, but I especially love your boisterous laugh because it's not what anyone would expect. You're the definition of graceful, so even though it might be unpleasant to others, it's like catnip to me." I nuzzle my beard against her sensitive neck and hold her close. She laughs loud and free.

Its everything.

The song changes, and we dance for a while, shaking our asses and being goofy as hell. I haven't laughed this much in years. Watching Grace hop on one foot as she spins around and around, I thank god she's here. That we're finally ready for this, and it's going to work because I won't survive if it doesn't.

"So, are we really going to drink that?"

"The absinthe? Hell yeah, we are. Just like old times, babe," I wink down at her before pulling her to the couch.

"Here, you can see I've got not only the elixir of our teenage memories but also a hookah from Willow."

"Is this memory lane? No, nightmare lane?" She laughs.

"Now, if you remember correctly, it wasn't all a nightmare."

"I don't know; that first time was horrifically embarrassing."

I scoff in mock horror as she did earlier. "Take that back! Do you not remember what I told you? I meant it. That didn't bother me, and it shouldn't bother you. It's natural for some virgins to bleed, and we both knew it would happen. I lasted all of five seconds, so really, I should be the embarrassed person in this scenario."

Her face turns earnest. "You're right. I take it back. It was a night I will never forget, and it wasn't all bad. I do remember my first orgasm."

"You better. I had licked so much fruit leading up to that trip, trying to make sure I would make you come." I feel the sly smile slide across my face at the memory. "My God, you were stunning."

Grace blushes. A sight not seen too often. Her smile is sweet and relaxed. She's totally at home in my apartment with me, in only my thin tee shirt. I lick my lips as my eyes sweep her body. My eyes are glued to her silhouette as she moves around, preparing the absinthe.

"I can't even remember how this tastes anymore, but I do remember hating it."

"It wasn't the taste you hated; you were pissed you didn't see tinker bell."

"Oh yeah. The creepy guy in the alley said we would see a little green fairy if we drank it."

She sets the sugar cube on top of the metal and lights it on fire. The small flame burns fast, but we both rear back in surprise. Laughing, she pushes my drink over to me. Before she sits back, I notice the shirt ride up her thigh and will myself not to reach out and find out if she put her thong back on or not. The thought has my dick hardening again.

"Those damn kids would believe anything," I joke.

"I think those two virgins just wanted an excuse to bang finally."

"You're not wrong, but that's not as romantic."

"It wasn't romantic."

"Wait," I say in mock surprise, touching my chest. "Are you telling me now that our first time together wasn't the fairy tale first time you always thought it would be? It was in a castle, Grace."

She laughs and rolls her eyes.

"A hostel is not a castle. Now I'm not saying our first time wasn't *magical*." She looks off towards the kitchen in thought. "We *were* high in a tall tower."

"With only each other to keep us warm."

"Amsterdam is cold."

I nod, encouraging her. "But it was magical…."

"Yes. Because that night, I gave myself to you, knowing and feeling you were giving all of you to me. It's not something I can put a word to, but *magical* comes close."

At this moment, if possible, I fall more in love with Grace Maddon.

## 7

# GRACE

*I* glance around the cold familiar hospital room anxiously waiting for Jake, I mean Dr. Williams. Unfortunately, I'm not interested in the most eligible doctor. Instead, I'm more excited to get out of here for a change. I officially get back to work next week, and Marcus went back to work today.

Tonight we tell Harmony that we're going on a date. Butterflies burst free, taking flight, and I hold my stomach with a smile. I've missed this excitement. I didn't realize it until now, but life has been such a dull, monotonous routine, but now that Marcus barged in and shook everything up, it's like I'm seeing in color for the first time. The world is brighter, and life seems so much easier. Even things like grocery shopping trips together have become something I enjoy instead of just another chore.

I want to be mad at myself for pushing him away for so long, but I wonder if we were ready six years ago. He was at the beginning of his career, and now it's in full swing. He spent six weeks away, caring for me and only checking in. Would he have done that for me back then? Probably not, because I know I wouldn't have let him.

We needed this time to grow our careers, and although I know we could have done that together, I think I would have grown bitter. It wouldn't have been fair to put my daddy issues on Marcus, but the truth is meeting my biological father and being so utterly disappointed did a number on me. Being so in love with Marcus consumed me before. Now I'm a different person. Stronger on my own, and I know my worth. Not that Marcus ever made me feel less than. If anything, he gently showed me how strong I am over these years. But I know in my bones we're stronger together.

"Grace. How is my favorite patient?" Dr. Williams asks, stepping into the small space. It seems to shrink as he comes in and stands so close to me I can smell the rubbing alcohol on his hands.

"Ready to be back on two legs and back to work."

As a trained nurse, I'm used to the smell, but him standing so close is new.

"We're ready to have you back. Sally Ann even wrote it on the back calendar, and a little birdie told me there's going to be donuts."

I laugh lightly, but my palms get sweaty when he puts his hands on my shoulders, forcing my full attention.

"I'm so glad you're ok. You really scared me."

"Um, thank you for your concern, but I'm fine."

"You're not fine, Grace. You need someone to take care of you. You do so much for everyone else, and you're clearly exhausted. I think you're the most selfless person I know, and you deserve someone good to come along and make everything better."

This is awkward. Does he know about Marcus and me? Marcus was in bed with me while I was in the hospital, and I know Dr. Williams noticed, but something about how he's using a softer bedroom voice confuses me. And he's too close…and touching me.

"Thank you, Doc, but I'm doing just fine." I try to push away the unease.

He steps back with a smile, but I can tell it's forced. My skin starts to crawl as I watch a more sinister expression cross his face. He runs his tongue over his front teeth as his eyes roam from my feet to my face.

"I can't wait to get this cast off you."

My eyes stay laser-focused on his back as he picks out the tools to needed saw my cast off. Suddenly I wish I could keep the stupid thing on and just leave. Dr. Jake Williams has always been a professional. Even the time he asked me out, I didn't feel pressured. He seemed like he assumed I wanted to, but he's gorgeous. I'm sure women fall at his feet.

I however am feeling uncomfortable.

Biting his bottom lip, he takes my cast and sits on the low stool. I take a deep breath with my guard up. I've never known him to be this casual or unprofessional.

I watch as he takes the cast saw and holds it to the top of the hardened pink wrap. It's painted with signatures and cute characters Willow and Harmony drew all over. If the thing wasn't a reminder of how I let my life spiral out of control, I might have wanted to keep it.

The steady blade begins cutting through the shell, causing a vibration against my leg but nothing more. Dr. Williams might be acting too casual, but his focus luckily stays on the job. Once he runs the saw down the inside of my leg, he grips it and creaks it open. It itches like crazy, and I know my leg hair must be a mile long, but suddenly with the change in his demeanor, I'm glad it's going to be gross.

"Almost free," he says, running a pair of professional scissors through the gauze. The cool air hits my skin and instantly erupts a trail of goosebumps. I'm free, and all I want to do is scratch. It's a gross mess of pressed hair and random fruit loops. He pushes away and turns to grab the wet rag.

"Thank you."

"You're welcome. I'll give you a moment."

He leaves, and I clean up. Glad I wore yoga pants.

Moments later, he's back. "You're all healed up."

"WONDERFUL." I can't help but smile, standing on two even feet again.

I walk a few steps and then stretch both legs out on the bed. This is the part where he's going to touch me. I'm surprised the thought isn't appealing, but it sours my stomach.

"How are things at home? Is Harmony helping out?"

"Yep," I answer simply.

"Now that is a perfect leg. You've healed as expected and shouldn't experience any long-term effects from the small fracture."

"Thank you."

He lingers well after clearing my physical wellness, and the hairs on the back of my neck stand up.

"Now we can finally go on that date you promised me." His tone is casual, and his smile is bright…but I never promised him anything.

"Oh gosh, I remember you asking me to dinner the night of the accident. I'm sorry I never gave you a firm answer when I said I'd think about it. The truth is, it's a very nice offer, but I'm not over my ex. You met him, Marcus, Harmony's Dad. We've recently started seeing each other again."

His casual smile falls, and his brows furrow. Suddenly a look of anger flashes across his face, but he quickly looks to the floor.

"Well then. I wish you both the best." Then he clears his throat and finally meets my eyes. "I hope we can still be friends."

"Um, sure. I will always be polite, Dr. Williams. Thank you again for helping me get back on my feet."

His jaw ticks when I say politely, but he straightens his back, seeming to go back into professional mode.

He washes his hands, and I slip into my shoes.

"Take care," I say, and with a wave to his back, I make my way out as fast as possible, which isn't too bad with this newly healed foot.

I meet my mom in the waiting room, and we head out to the car. On the drive home, I keep thinking that I've never felt uncomfortable around Dr. Williams before, but I could tell he didn't like being turned down. Taking a deep breath and turning up the radio, I check my messages.

**Marcus: Dinner is being catered by Lyla. Mac and Cheese, burgers, sweet potato fries, and fried pickles.**

Harmony's favorite. Tonight's a big night, and he's buttering her up. It's sweet that he's nervous, but I have a good feeling about her reaction. I think she'll be thrilled and say something snarky.

**Me: Sounds amazing. Tonight is going to be perfect.**

When I get home, I'm greeted with a big hug.

"Missed you, mama bear."

"Missed you too, baby bear. Happy to be home."

"Where's Grandma?"

"She needed to get back to Grandpa Dean. He was missing her. But she told me to tell you that she will be here bright and early to take you to the beach."

"Yay! Do I get to go in the RV?"

"Yeah, sure." I laugh at her priorities.

"Hey you," Marcus says, coming around the corner, slinging a kitchen towel over his shoulder. His black dress pants hug his thick muscular thighs, and I enjoy watching him as he moves in to hug me. We keep it innocent, but our smiles are sly and knowing.

We've always been a close family. Even though Marcus and I haven't been a couple, we co-parent seamlessly, but it's incredible how easy it is to get along with someone you've always been in love with.

"Dinner is ready, ladies."

"It smells so good." Harmony and I say in unison. We are fortunate to know Lyla, who is a world-renowned chef and loves to show her love with food. Very few people know that she loves to cook so much because when she was younger, her mom was too busy to even cook for her. My friend is amazing and beat the odds not only growing up, where she put herself through culinary school, but when she thought she had lost everything a couple of years ago, she rebuilt her reputation and settled back home here in sunny San Diego. I hardly ever cook, and when I do, it's usually one of Mom's classic crock pot meals, which Lyla's better at making. But her cooking for my family now and then is a treat because I'm more than happy to eat her exquisite meals. Hell, I eat lunch or breakfast at her small eatery downtown. The beloved record store she restored and flipped into a place of her own.

The kitchen table is set with my navy-blue runner and plastic eucalyptus and a feast for three that squeezes my heart. This is one of those moments I'll never forget. It might be a little thing to most, but this means so much to me, and I know it must be the same for Harmony because it's been just the two of us for so long. If it wasn't the two of us, it was the two of them, and now we're going to put our pieces back together. Tonight is a night that our lives as we know it will change …for the better.

"Slow down, champ," Marcus tells his daughter as she chews on a huge bite of delicious macaroni and cheese. We all have a good laugh as it drips down her chin.

Our meal is delicious, and when it's time to clean up, the three of us dance to Harmony's approved playlist tunes. Us girls can't help but giggle as Marcus belts out the Taylor Swift lyrics. Our little girl twirls as she takes the plates to the sink, and I shake my awkward butt around, wiping down the counters. The chore goes by quickly, and we decide to settle into a family movie.

"Frozen!"

"No!" Marcus and I both shout as she grabs the remote.

"Okay, okay, sheesh," she laughs.

While she lists a few more movie titles, I pull some blankets and extra pillows from the hallway closet. My leg feels weak but solid as I move around.

Settling onto our respective sides of the couch, Harmony pushes play on Beauty and Beast. With the same remote, she dims the lights, and I look over to find Marcus giving me *the* look. You know, the one that parents use to communicate secretly. This one is telling me it's time we have this talk with her.

"So, baby girl," I watch him run his palm over her cheek as she stares up at him with so much adoration it hurts. "We have something we want to talk to you about before we start the movie. Is that ok?"

"Sure Daddy. What's up?" She asks, pressing pause at the Disney castle intro.

He takes an audible breath. "I would really like to take Mama Bear to dinner and dancing and stuff like that. It turns out we've both been missing each other and wishing we hung out more."

"Like a date?"

"Yeah, that's what I'm thinkin'. Lots of dates." Marcus grins at me when he says the last part.

Maybe I should be more worried about the repercussions of telling her this now and not a few months down the road. But there isn't any negative what if's clouding my judgment. I know with my whole heart this is right.

"Oh, I would love that. Can I come, or are these dates like the mommy daddy dates my friends' parents take without them?"

I laugh wholeheartedly.

"It'll just be mommy and me for the dates, but mommy and I were thinking that maybe I shouldn't move back to my house but stay here instead."

"Oh yes! That's a great idea! You can move your stuff into mommy's room. Your big dresser with all your fancy watches will fit in there. Mommy doesn't have as many clothes as you do, so there's gonna be plenty of space in the closet, and the best part is you have your own bathroom."

Marcus blinks rapidly at Harmony after her big speech.

"Why do you think I should move into mommy's room?"

"Well, because Mommy's in there. You guys can snuggle all night long."

"Willow and Archer let her watch Little Italy at their last sleepover. It faded to black, and she explained to Harmony that they were cuddling."

He nods with a tight smile, obviously trying hard not to laugh at our daughter's innocence.

"That's right, sweetheart. Does that sound like a good plan to you?"

"The best plan. I just want to have one room 'cause I keep leaving something I need in my other room and my friends at school don't understand 'cause they only have one room and one house with their mommy and daddy. Honestly, I didn't want to mention it, but it's kind of weird. I'm glad we'll be in one place all together."

He shakes his head, stunned at her casual response.

"Our very mature daughter here knows we've always been a family. We were just being weird by living apart. Imagine that," I say with a shrug of my shoulder and kiss her forehead. Marcus leans over her head and kisses me. It's the first time we've ever shown affection in front of her, and all she does is press play on her movie. I know my over-opinionated daughter is just as happy about this new dynamic as we are, but not much about our day-to-day lives will change, and what does change will only make us happier.

8

---

# MARCUS

*A* cold burst of air greets me as I walk through the hospital doors of Scripps Memorial Hospital. My Grace is here, and I can't wait to kiss her.

I wave politely to the ladies behind the desk in the large lobby. They know me from years of picking up Harmony, so they smile with a matching wink when they see my arms full of flowers and takeout. The elevator doors are open, so I quickly rush in and push the button for the tenth floor. The place is quiet when I step off.

"Hey, ladies." I smile at the gaggle of nurses, and they wave.

Nearing the end of a long hallway, I hear an angry male voice. I wonder for a moment if a rowdy patient is giving my Grace a hard time, but when I turn to peep inside, I drop the bag and flowers and barge into the room so fast the fuckers head spins. My fist is up and ready, and my blood is boiling as the good Dr. Williams crowds a very uncomfortable Grace.

I watch as he quickly rights himself, but it's too late; I see red, my fist starts to swing, but Grace slides out from between him and the wall and rushes me.

"Baby, stop! Trust me!" She shouts.

I hear the strength in her voice, and I know my woman is strong. If

56

she says to stop, I won't hit him…at least not yet. I make a last-minute move that only leaves him scared. My fist connects with the wall next to him as I snarl in his pathetic face.

"What the fuck do you think you're doing?"

Dr. Dumbass clenches his jaw. He wants to hit me, say all the right things, and stay the big shot everyone thinks he is. I know better. His eyes tell me he's shitting his pants at being caught harassing someone. **My someone.** I grit my teeth but step back when her soft hand squeezes my shoulder.

"Grace and I were just having a conversation. Nothing to be too jealous about…yet." He tells me with a cocky grin.

"Or ever. Like I was explaining to you, yet again, Dr. Williams. I'm happily reunited with the love of my life. In fact, I absolutely will not miss your uncomfortable advances when you're gone."

He pauses for a moment, seeming to think over his next move while scratching his chin with his thumb in deep thought.

"Sally Ann, did you get all that?"

Just then, the woman steps out of the nearby bathroom. One that had been cracked open and had a great view of everything that just transpired. An evil grin slides across her face as Grace nods and crosses her arms. This was a setup, and these amazing women were brave enough to pull it off.

"I got every word. Thanks for the backup, Marcus," Sally Ann says with a smile, and suddenly, security flanks the entrance, making the once prideful doctor start stuttering.

"You got to be kidding me with this shit. Don't touch me. Do you know who I am? I make more than all three of you combined. I said don't fucking touch me. I demand to talk to the Chief Physician. It's fucking lies!" He shouts the last part over his shoulder as he's forcefully removed from the room.

"Oh, you will, don't worry." The older nurse Salley Ann shouts.

"You sent her the video," Grace asks Sally Ann as I take her in my arms for a much needed embrace. God, that was scary. My heart is still racing as I rock her in my arms. She laughs lightly and pats my back.

"Do you mean did I forward an email with the video to everyone that has the power to destroy his career? Including the good Chief Physician, Melanie Arvato, yes I did."

We all have a good laugh, and several people rush in to ask what was happening. That started an even bigger conversation about the women being harassed by Dr. Williams and several of the men on staff in the hospital.

"Ladies, I think we can all say today was a win," Grace says as a few nurses have to back out of the room to care for patients but nod their support. I have no doubt the events of today and the ones to come will spread through this hospital like wildfire. The power of that movement gave me an idea.

"But this was just one of many toxic people in power in this hospital."

"Grace, I have an idea. May I?" I ask her, stepping forward to address the room. I remind myself to consider everyone's feelings when I ask this. They all have families to feed…but some might have daughters like mine. When my love smiles at me, giving me the ok, I look around the room, making eye contact with everyone giving me the attention I don't deserve on this subject. The tension is thick as I clear my throat.

"You all worked hard to earn the jobs you do day in and day out. With blood of your own, sweat and tears from family members who miss you because you work all the time." That gets me a few laughs. "No one deserves to feel stuck in a job they're uncomfortable going to. That's bullshit. I don't work here and don't know half of your stories, but if you tell me, I promise I'll use my power in the entertainment industry to make sure your voice is heard. My daughter is six and fiercely independent…just like her mom. I don't want her to grow up in a world where women don't get treated with the respect they deserve, and I want to be part of the change we can make for the better."

The room starts cheering, but I shake my head and laugh. More women have crowded into the room now, and I notice lots of glistening stares.

Reaching into my pocket, I pull out my business card.

"This is my office address and personal cell phone number. Sit down with me for as long as it takes. I'll have a box of tissues, a camera, and zero judgment about what you choose to tell me. If you decide to tell me your story, I'll make a collaborative video for the world to see. And you can trust me, ladies; the world will see it."

Everyone agrees, and one by one, I meet several women with stories to tell. They all thank me and promise to be in touch. I have no idea what time Grace and I finally make our way home. We had to make a formal complaint and email a few more people the video.

Closing the front door to our home, I take a long breath of relief. I'm grateful she's ok, and he didn't hurt her. I'm also proud as hell.

"I'm so damn proud of you, woman," I tell her, taking her in my arms.

"I would like to say the same thing, "Mr. Tell-me-your-story. That is so gracious of you. Thank you for using your voice for us."

"Of course. I meant every word I said. I'm scared for our daughter in this world as it is right now. We have this chance, thanks to you," I say, kissing her nose. "to truly make a difference, and I'd be honored to be a part of that change for the better."

"My god, you're sexy when you talk so respectfully," she says, then lifts to her toes and bites my lip.

I groan as my cock grows hard from the pain. A sharp sting that's oddly thrilling. Her playful laugh fills my ears. Grabbing her waist, I pull her firmly against my aching need. Her light laughter turns to a moan. I relish it. My mouth dives down her neck. I suck on her sweet skin as I back her up to the apartment's floor-to-ceiling windows. When she is firmly pressed against the glass, I lift her shirt. Kiss her collar bone. Run my hands slowly down her soft hips, thighs, and legs, taking her pants down to the floor where she steps out of them. I kiss her knee, stopping my rise to admire her glistening pussy. She's waxed and needy. Slowly I taste her. My tongue lit up at her sweet flavor. She moans for me, bucking into my face as I devour her. I want her wild and loose and to take whatever she wants. Pushing two fingers inside her, I pump them. Hard punishing strokes as I play the tip of my tongue across her clit.

"Oh god, baby, too good. Fuck, so good."

My love gets too sensitive sometimes, and I've learned to read her queues like the daily news.

I stop and pull out after a few slow strokes. Standing, I tower over my naked Grace.

"I love you, Grace. I'm honored to be yours, and I cherish you as mine." I take her mouth in a chaste kiss pressing my erection against her belly. "Now turn around because I want the world to watch me fuck you, and know that you're mine. That the kind, beautiful, badass fucking queen who took down her aggressor today is coming on my cock and yelling my name."

She turns around to face the glass window. The windows are all designed with a tint so no one can see us…but the thrill is still there.

I take off my belt, strip off my shirt, pants, and boxers, and stand behind my girl raw. Bending a bit, I rub my thick girth up her crack. Her back arches and her ass eagerly presses against me. Finding her wrists, I take them and hold them against the glass above her head. Taking that control, so she's free to clear her mind and enjoy every ounce of pleasure I give her.

"This is it, baby. You're my forever, you hear me. I'm claiming you for all to see. Let them watch our passion as I fuck you."

"Yes."

My fingers inch their way to her clit. I rub her, making her scream. The sound is music to my ears. I watch my cock slide into her slick pussy as I pound harder.

When she screams my name and I explode. My love, desire, respect, loyalty, and friendship all pour into her as my release breaks. She screams my name as she shakes with her own orgasm. I release her wrists and cradle her until we both catch our breath. Then gently, I carry her to my bed.

"God, you're amazing." She says, staring at me. We've cleaned up and crawled into bed. Harmony is spending the night with my Mom and Declan, and I plan on making love to this beautiful woman on every surface. Making up for lost time has become a game we play, and I don't see it ever getting old.

"I love you. I can't help but turn beast when I'm inside you."

"Beast is a great word for it, and I loved it. I love you."

Her soft hand runs over my face, and I close my eyes.

"This is our happily ever after. I want to make you feel good."

"You're doing a great job, Marcus. I've never been happier."

Her words hit me hard, and I kiss her with all the adoration I feel. This is what we wanted all those years ago, and now we finally get to live it.

Our happily ever after…our forever…is starting again.

The End

# ABOUT THE AUTHOR

Heather Lauren is a polly pocket size mom of three who only takes her book boyfriends seriously. She lives in sunny Arizona and enjoys writing steamy contemporary romance and romantic comedies with a strong cup of coffee or a sweet cocktail in hand. Listen along to your favorite book characters on the made for you playlists on Spotify and watch out for Easter eggs in all her books.

# OTHER BOOKS BY HEATHER LAUREN

https://www.amazon.com/Heather-Lauren/e/B08LH8XSLZ/ref=
aufs_dp_fta_dsk

**Rum and Records (free)**

https://storyoriginapp.com/giveaways/77ac4402-396f-11eb-8e2e-
d3776136d48e

**Whiskey and Honey**

https://www.amazon.ca/dp/B08Q4JNFJ3

**Black Velvet and Lace**

https://www.amazon.ca/dp/B08VJLH7WV

**Vodka and Pop Rocks**

https://www.amazon.ca/dp/B096YZQ82Z

**Absinthe and Heart**

https://www.amazon.ca/dp/B09C2MHB8J

**Socially Awkward Series-**

https://www.amazon.ca/dp/B0925P246S

**Un-Swipe: an enemies to lovers romantic comedy**

https://www.amazon.ca/dp/B09257CP8D

**Un-Like: an unrequited love/fake date romantic comedy**

https://www.amazon.ca/dp/B0973JF932

**Un-Friend: a secret baby/road trip romantic comedy**

https://www.goodreads.com/author/show/20801651.Heather_Lauren

Interconnected Standalones

Bourbon Backroads

(Dean & Sawyer's story Graces mom and step dad)

https://www.amazon.ca/dp/B09PRQZMBW


Curves For Christmas Series

The Holiday Set Up

https://www.amazon.ca/dp/B09895R35B

Single Dad Santa

https://www.amazon.ca/dp/B0B4MCC9XR


Holidates Series

Falling For My Holidate

(Dominic and Sophie's Story)

https://www.amazon.ca/dp/B09GNSGCBJ


Bred and Butter: Baby Breeder

https://www.amazon.ca/dp/B0B57WGKNN


Man of the Month Club Series Books

Beards and Books

https://www.amazon.ca/dp/B08X16J98Z

Beards and Love Letters

https://www.amazon.ca/dp/B09LBJFQCK


Coming Soon

Strong Man: Night Circus Series


Thank you so much for taking the time to read my story. This was a love story very near to my heart because it is the last book in the Empire Records Series, and is my first series completed. Its bitter sweet. I think I could have made Marcus and Graces' story three times as long. With all the family dynamics changing the pace of the crew of friends and side characters I've fallen in love with I could have just kept going forever but I hope you are happy with the very end of the Empire Records Series. Be on the look out for all the those side characters I love so much though because I've already started giving them there own stories. Dane Carmichal from Whiskey and Honey and Black Velvet and Lace is Sophie Carmichaels brother in Falling For My Holidate and he's getting his HEA in Bred and Butter.

*Insider secret: The Wallflowers and Headspace will all be getting there own books :) ssshh don't tell but be sure to stay in touch ;)

xoxo

Heather

www.heatherlaurenbooks.com

Lets stay in touch! Join my newsletter and get the prequel to The Empire Records Series, Nora nd Declans love story Free! https://storyoriginapp.com/giveaways/77ac4402-396f-11eb-8e2e-d3776136d48e

Love you bye.

www.ingramcontent.com/pod-product-compliance
Lightning Source LLC
Chambersburg PA
CBHW061712130726
47996CB00006B/2267